Collins

TUNNEL OF TERROR

Barry Hutchison

Illustrated by
Ciaran Duffy

Jim shivered. It was October and it was nearly midnight. It was the first time he'd been out so late without his parents. He'd crept out without telling them. As far as his mum and dad knew, he was safely tucked up in bed. He was beginning to wish that he was.

He stared up at a sign above the entrance to a fairground ride. The writing was faded and the metal was rusty. The ride itself wasn't much better. Paint flaked off the walls and some of the wood looked rotten.

"I thought it was supposed to be brand new," Jim said.

Jim's best friend, Karl, stood beside him. Karl was taller than Jim, and sportier too. He ran or cycled everywhere. Jim was the opposite. He never hurried anywhere and preferred playing FIFA on the computer to playing football in real life. Despite their differences, the two boys had been friends for as long as they could remember.

"It is new. That's all just for effect," Karl replied. He caught Jim by the arm and pulled him towards the entrance.

A small crowd had gathered around the ride. Jim tried to stop near the back, but Karl pulled him on until they were right at the front. The painted walls of the ride loomed above them.

"So what do you reckon it is, then?" Karl asked.

They had heard about the Tunnel of Terror almost two months ago. Some friends from school had told them about it. No one knew what it was, but everyone had heard the rumour that it was going to open at midnight on Halloween.

Tonight was Halloween and there were just a few minutes left until midnight. The Tunnel of Terror was about to open for business.

Karl was hopping from foot to foot. Jim didn't know if he was excited or just trying to keep warm.

"I was hoping for a rollercoaster," Karl said. "But it isn't one of them."

"It's a ghost train," Jim said.

"What? How do you know?" Karl asked.

Jim pointed to one of the rotten walls. "Because it's written up there."

Karl read the faded lettering. "Tunnel of Terror Ghost Train," he mumbled. "Well, that's rubbish."

"Why? What's wrong with ghost trains?" Jim asked.

"What's *right* with ghost trains? They're boring."

Jim shrugged. "Maybe we should just go home, then." He secretly hoped Karl would agree. He was worried what would happen if his mum and dad found out he was gone.

"No way. We're here now," Karl said. "We may as well go for it."

Before Jim could argue, the door at the front of the ride opened. A tall and skinny man in a top hat hobbled out. He had a hooked nose like a bird's beak and eyes that were almost black. He carried a wooden cane that was nearly as tall as he was. At the top of the cane was a life-sized human skull.

The man banged the cane three times on the wooden floor. The crowd fell silent as they waited to hear what he was going to say.

Chapter 2

The man with the skull cane took a watch from his pocket, looked at it, then put it away again.

"Good evening, brave souls," he said. "My name is Randus Hex. Welcome to my Tunnel of Terror. I promise that this will be the most frightening ride of your lives."

"Yeah, right," Karl mumbled. Randus Hex turned his head and stared at the two boys. His mouth curved into a nasty smile. Jim shuffled nervously and stepped back behind his friend.

The watch in Randus Hex's pocket began to chime. His eyes sparkled and his smile became wider. "Midnight is upon us," he announced. He beckoned to some of the closest adults. "Enter the Tunnel of Terror and prepare to scream … for your lives!"

Once the first few adults had gone in, Karl pulled Jim into the queue. The skull on Randus Hex's cane seemed to watch them as they filed through the door.

On the other side of the door was a narrow platform beside some rusty rail tracks. The tracks disappeared through a door that had been painted to look like a screaming ghost.

"This is so lame," Karl said.

A car was just leaving the platform when Jim and Karl arrived. A man and a woman were sitting in it, a metal safety bar across their legs. They laughed nervously as the car gathered speed along the tracks and through the ghost-faced door.

Another door opened at the other end of the platform. A car shot through and stopped right in front of Jim and Karl.

"It's empty," Jim said.

"Yeah, so?"

"Well … where did the people go? Isn't this the only way off and on?"

Karl shrugged. "They probably got off somewhere else." He jumped down into the car. "Now come on, let's get this over with."

Jim hopped in beside him. The metal safety bar locked into place across their legs. The car shot forwards suddenly, pushing them back in their seat. Somewhere nearby, Jim heard a scream. He gripped the metal bar as the car rushed towards the ghost-faced door.

"Here we go," Karl said. He nudged Jim with his elbow. "If you pee yourself, try to keep it on your own side."

The door opened. The car crashed through, and everything around them went dark.

Chapter 3

Fake cobwebs tickled Jim's face. He brushed them away in time to see a plastic zombie light up on the wall.

"Ooh, scary," Karl said.

"Yeah, if you're three years old," Jim snorted.

A recording of a werewolf howl crackled from a hidden speaker and made Jim jump in his seat.

Karl laughed. "You're such a wimp!"

"It just caught me by surprise, that's all," Jim replied.

He gripped the bar even more tightly as the car turned a corner. More cobwebs hit him in the face. A coffin door creaked open and a cardboard vampire popped out. A white sheet with a face painted on it dropped from the ceiling on a spring.

"You were right, this *is* lame," Jim said. "I can't believe we risked getting grounded for this."

The car jerked round another bend. A green light flashed on and the boys saw a row of skeletons dangling from the wall by their hands. Their skulls seemed to grin as the car crept past.

"They were pretty good," Jim admitted, as the light went out again. "They looked almost real."

Another scream echoed along the dark passageway. This time both boys jumped. "That one sounded better," Karl said.

"Yeah," Jim nodded, and a cold breeze tickled his neck. "They sounded really scared, didn't they?"

Karl didn't answer. The only sound in the tunnel was the creaking of the car along the track.

"Don't you think?" Jim said.

Karl still didn't answer.

"Karl?"

Jim reached through the darkness. Where he expected to find his friend, he found only empty space. His stomach went tight with fear as he realised he was alone in the car.

Karl was gone!

The car began to move faster. Jim gripped the bar so tightly his knuckles turned white.

"Karl?" he cried. "Where are you?"

It didn't make sense. The bar had not moved. There was no way Karl should have been able to get out. But he had. Somehow, he had.

A light flashed, casting the shadow of a man with a skull-topped cane across the wall. A voice whispered from the gloom. "Get ready for a surprise ..."

Strange shapes suddenly appeared in the darkness on either side of the tracks. Freakish men and women with bulging eyes, long tongues and crooked noses stepped from the shadows.

The shapes clawed at Jim as he shot past. He thought at first they must be plastic or cardboard. Then he screamed. They were *real*. They were *all real*! Only the chains around their necks stopped them getting to him.

The car turned a sharp corner, then came to a sudden stop. Jim screamed again as the car tilted forwards and he was tipped out onto the track. He only just managed to jump out of the way before the car raced forwards again. It clanked off along the tracks, leaving him completely alone in the dark.

"H-hello?" he said. "Is … is anyone there?"

He heard a low giggle from somewhere nearby. Panic made his legs start moving. He stumbled through the dark, feeling with his hands. There had to be a way out. There *had* to be!

More cobwebs snagged on his face. He pulled them away and kept running as fast as he dared. He yelped with fright as he ran straight into a wall.

Jim turned sharply in another direction, but found a wall there, too.

Feeling around him, Jim realised there were walls on three sides. It was a dead end! Behind him he heard the giggle again. Footsteps scuffed along the floor towards him. A shape moved in the shadows.

"Who's there?" Jim whimpered. "Stop this. I want to get out."

The shape in the darkness didn't answer him. It just crept closer and closer, nearer and nearer.

Suddenly, Jim heard Karl's voice. He was screaming for help and sounded somewhere off to the left. Jim felt further along the wall and found the handle of a door. As quickly as he could, he opened it and darted through.

The room on the other side glowed with a spooky green light. Skeletons hung from the walls. Jim approached them slowly. Were these the same skeletons he had seen earlier?

Up close, they looked even more realistic. On some of them, the bones were old and yellow. A few of the others looked newer, with bones that were still white.

Jim turned away from the skeleton at the end of the line. Tiny scraps of flesh and hair still clung to it. A smell of rotting meat caught in Jim's throat and almost made him choke.

"Karl?" he coughed. "Are you in here?"

"Jim! I'm over here! Help me down!"

Jim followed his friend's voice. He gasped when he saw that Karl was chained to the wall, just along from the row of skeletons. Jim hurried to Karl's side and tried to remove the chains.

"I can't get them off," Jim said. "They're stuck."

"Well get them *unstuck* then! Get me out of here. This place stinks. I swear I'm going to throw up. What is that smell?"

Jim looked at the skeleton hanging along the wall from Karl. It was chained up exactly like his friend was. The smell was coming from it, and from all the other skeletons hanging from the wall. Jim knew that could only mean one thing.

"Dead bodies," Jim whispered. "It's the smell of dead bodies. These skeletons aren't fake."

Even in the green light, Jim saw Karl's face go pale. "G-get me out," Karl cried. "Hurry!"

Jim nodded and set to work trying to free his friend. The chains were heavy and held in place with thick metal bands around Karl's wrists. Jim tugged and pulled, but the chains held tight.

Jim was so busy with the chains that he didn't hear the door creaking open behind him. He didn't hear the footsteps shuffling across the floor. He didn't hear the soft giggle, until a hand clamped over his mouth and something sharp was stuck into his neck.

"Jim, no!" Karl screamed, but he sounded far away.

Jim's head went fuzzy and he dropped to his knees. He heard the rattle of chains as they were pulled tight around his wrists.

"You see?" whispered Randus Hex in his ear. "I told you this would be the most frightening ride of your lives. And it's going to be the last one, too."

Jim heard the giggle again. He heard Karl begin to cry. And then he heard nothing at all, as the world went dark and he fell into a deep, dreamless sleep.

Reader challenge

Word hunt

1 On page 13, find an adjective that means "mean".

2 On page 25, find an adjective that means "bent".

3 On page 36, find a noun that means "laugh".

Story sense

4 How do you think Jim felt when he found Karl's seat was empty? (page 23)

5 Who was following Jim in the dark? How do you know? (pages 28–29)

6 Why do you think Jim approached the skeletons slowly? (page 31)

7 Why did Karl's face go pale? (page 35)

8 What was the last thing Jim heard before he fell into a deep sleep? (page 37)

Your views

9 Do you think Jim was a "wimp" or not? Give reasons.

10 Do you think Jim believed he could free Karl? Give reasons.

Spell it

With a partner, look at these words and then cover them up.

- scream
- creak
- dream

Take it in turns for one of you to read the words aloud. The other person has to try and spell each word. Check your answers, then swap over.

Try it

Play the describing game. With a partner, think of as many words as you can to describe the Tunnel of Terror ride. Take it in turns to give each other a word. When one person can't think of anything else to say, or a word is repeated, they lose the game.

William Collins's dream of knowledge for all began with the publication of his first book in 1819. A self-educated mill worker, he not only enriched millions of lives, but also founded a flourishing publishing house. Today, staying true to this spirit, Collins books are packed with inspiration, innovation and practical expertise. They place you at the centre of a world of possibility and give you exactly what you need to explore it.

Collins. Freedom to teach.

Published by Collins Education
An imprint of HarperCollins*Publishers*
77–85 Fulham Palace Road
Hammersmith
London
W6 8JB

Browse the complete Collins Education catalogue at **www.collinseducation.com**

Text by Barry Hutchison © HarperCollins Publishers Limited 2012
Illustrations by Ciaran Duffy © HarperCollins Publishers Limited 2012

Series consultants: Alan Gibbons and Natalie Packer

10 9 8 7 6 5 4 3 2 1
ISBN 978-0-00-746476-0

British Library Cataloguing in Publication Data.
A catalogue record for this publication is available from the British Library.

Commissioned by Catherine Martin
Edited and project-managed by Sue Chapple
Illustration management by Tim Satterthwaite
Proofread by Grace Glendinning
Design and typesetting by Jordan Publishing Design Limited
Cover design by Paul Manning

Acknowledgements

The publishers would like to thank the students and teachers of the following schools for their help in trialling the Read On series:

Southfields Academy, London
Queensbury School, Queensbury, Bradford
Langham C of E Primary School, Langham, Rutland
Ratton School, Eastbourne, East Sussex
Northfleet School for Girls, North Fleet, Kent
Westergate Community School, Chichester, West Sussex
Bottesford C of E Primary School, Bottesford, Nottinghamshire
Woodfield Academy, Redditch, Worcestershire
St Richard's Catholic College, Bexhill, East Sussex